Demon Teddy

NICHOLAS ALLAN

HUTCHINSON
London Sydney Auckland Johannesburg

To Amanda

First published in 1999
1 3 5 7 9 10 8 6 4 2

First published in the United Kingdom in 1999 by
Hutchinson Children's Books
Random House UK Limited
20 Vauxhall Bridge Road, London SW1V 2SA

Random House Australia (Pty) Limited
20 Alfred Street, Milsons Point, Sydney
New South Wales 2061, Australia

Random House New Zealand Limited
18 Poland Road, Glenfield
Auckland 10, New Zealand

Random House South Africa (Pty) Limited
Endulini, 5A Jubilee Road, Parktown 2193, South Africa

Random House UK Limited Reg. No. 954009

A CIP catalogue record for this book
is available from the British Library

ISBN: 0 09 176943 4

Printed in Singapore

Katie was a shy little girl.

Dominic said she was stupid.

Dominic was a sneaky little boy.
But Miss Bird thought he was perfect.

Katie knew the right answers,
but wasn't always sure ...
Dominic was sure of everything.

Katie was often lonely.

One day she bought a wonderful

Toy Shop

teddy bear who talked to her.

She took him to school.
Dominic said she was soppy.

That day was Miss Bird's birthday.
She had a new bag.

'Please, Miss Bird,' said Dominic, 'can you show us your new –'

–went Fluffy suddenly, and everyone thought it was Dominic.

The Head gave Miss Bird a huge bunch of flowers.

'Gosh, Miss Bird,' said Dominic, 'you've got a great big –'

–went Fluffy, and everyone thought it was Dominic.

Later Miss Bird asked, 'If a man eats ten cakes and then eats ninety cakes, what would that make?'

'Please, Miss Bird.' Dominic put up his hand. 'It'd make –'

–went Fluffy, and everyone thought it was Dominic.

Dominic didn't dare say another word. So Katie did.

'Well done, Katie,' Miss Bird said.

That afternoon was the school outing.
Katie told some jokes and everyone laughed.

And soon she had

lots of friends.

So Dominic decided, with Fluffy's help, he'd
teach them all a lesson.

Dominic said, 'I think you lot are all a load of –'

ANGELS

–went Fluffy, and everyone thought it was Dominic.
'What a sweet boy,' they said.

When it was time to clear up Miss Bird asked,
'Who's going to help?'

Dominic said, 'I'm not –'

BUSY!

–went Fluffy, and everyone thought it was Dominic.
'Sweet, kind boy,' they all said.

And before long Dominic had some friends too.

But then Katie saw Dominic with Fluffy.

'Give him back,' she cried.

'No!' he said.

So she hit him.

–went Fluffy, and
Dominic thought it
was Katie.

–went Fluffy, and
Katie thought it
was Dominic.

So Katie said, 'Will you be my friend?'
And Dominic said, 'Well, all right.'
And Katie said, 'Shall we go and play then?'
And Dominic said, 'Yes, let's go and play.'

And this time Fluffy didn't have to say anything at all.